Pete and Penny's
PIZZA PU

Case of the Topsy-Turvy Toy

by Aaron Rosenberg
illustrated by David Harrington

PSS!
PRICE STERN SLOAN
An Imprint of Penguin Group (USA) Inc.

For Adara and Arthur, who constantly puzzle and delight me—AR

To my adorable nieces, Elise and Sabrina—DH

PRICE STERN SLOAN
Published by the Penguin Group
Penguin Group (USA) Inc., 375 Hudson Street, New York, New York 10014, USA
Penguin Group (Canada), 90 Eglinton Avenue East, Suite 700,
Toronto, Ontario M4P 2Y3, Canada
(a division of Pearson Penguin Canada Inc.)
Penguin Books Ltd., 80 Strand, London WC2R 0RL, England
Penguin Group Ireland, 25 St. Stephen's Green, Dublin 2, Ireland
(a division of Penguin Books Ltd.)
Penguin Group (Australia), 250 Camberwell Road, Camberwell,
Victoria 3124, Australia
(a division of Pearson Australia Group Pty. Ltd.)
Penguin Books India Pvt. Ltd., 11 Community Centre,
Panchsheel Park, New Delhi—110 017, India
Penguin Group (NZ), 67 Apollo Drive, Rosedale, North Shore 0632, New Zealand
(a division of Pearson New Zealand Ltd.)
Penguin Books (South Africa) (Pty.) Ltd., 24 Sturdee Avenue,
Rosebank, Johannesburg 2196, South Africa

Penguin Books Ltd., Registered Offices:
80 Strand, London WC2R 0RL, England

ISBN 978-0-8431-9929-1   10 9 8 7 6 5 4 3 2 1

Chapter One

"Pete! Penny!" Mr. Pizzarelli called. "Slices are up for tables four and sixteen!"

"Coming, Dad!" Penny checked to make sure her apron was still tied properly and hurried back toward the counter. Her younger brother, Pete, was right behind her.

Most nights their mom and dad could handle the dinner crowd at Pizzarelli's Pizza Parlor. But tonight was extra busy, so Pete and Penny were helping out. They took orders. They brought drinks and silverware to tables. They carried money to the counter and brought change to customers.

Steve, Pete's friend from school, was eating there tonight. "Hey!" Steve called as Pete walked by with the slices for table four. "Too bad you're working today." They were off from school for Fall Break and Steve thought it would have been fun to hang out with Pete.

Pete smiled and said, "You're just jealous you can't be *this* close to pizza all the time!"

Steve laughed.

Even though Pete was only nine years old, he liked working at the pizza place. Penny did, too. Lots of Redville residents ate at Pizzarelli's more than once a week. Pete and Penny knew everyone in town.

"Wow, there are a lot of new people here tonight!" Penny commented as she and Pete walked into the kitchen. "What's that about?"

"People do come from all over for our top secret sauce!" Mrs. Pizzarelli reminded them. She was tall and blond. Penny, who was eleven, looked like her.

"That's not why it's extra busy here *tonight*, though," Mr. Pizzarelli added. "Today was the first day of the Topsy-Turvy Toys Toy Fair."

Penny nodded. That explained all the extra people. Every booth was full. There was even a line for seats.

The Topsy-Turvy Toys company was in Garden City. It held a big toy fair each year.

The fair was a four-day convention for toy makers and toy store owners. People could show off new toys and talk about how to make and sell toys better. Penny knew that Garden City was too small for the fair. That's why they chose to hold it in Redville.

"Hey, can you two come help make this pie?" Mr. Pizzarelli broke into Penny's thoughts. He set a plain pizza down on the kitchen counter.

Penny's face lit up. "Sweet!" They didn't usually get to help make pizzas. Pete and Penny sat down on two stools at the counter. Pete's feet dangled above the floor.

Mr. Pizzarelli brought over two small bowls. He set them in front of Pete and Penny. "This pizza should have mushrooms on one half and black olives on the other," he said.

The black olives were closest to Penny. She grabbed the bowl and started to toss black olives onto her side of the pizza.

"Not so fast," Mr. Pizzarelli said, ruffling Pete's dark hair. "You can't just throw the toppings on there."

Pete looked at his half and then at the bowl

of mushrooms. "How many do we need to use then?" he asked.

Mr. Pizzarelli thought for a second. Then he said, "Pete, you need to add as many mushrooms as Penny's age. Penny, add as many olives as your age plus Pete's age put together."

Pete and Penny grinned. "A puzzle!" They loved puzzles. All the Pizzarellis did! In fact, they were such good puzzle solvers that everyone in town knew about their skills. Townspeople sometimes even asked for their help!

Pete and Penny got right to work on the pizza puzzle.

(Answer, page 62.)

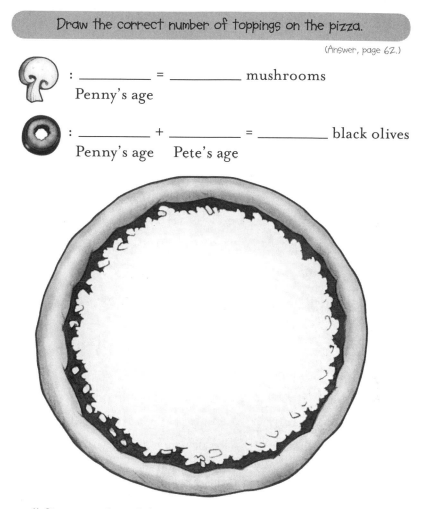

: _____ = _____ mushrooms
Penny's age

: _____ + _____ = _____ black olives
Penny's age   Pete's age

"Great job adding toppings, kids!" said
Mr. Pizzarelli. He placed the pizza in the oven.
   "Check, please!" someone called. Pete and
Penny hopped off their stools to get back to work.

Chapter Two

The next night, Pete and Penny were in the kitchen helping their mom prepare for the dinner crowd. They were refilling the small, glass jars that held parmesan cheese.

"Well, well," Mr. Pizzarelli said. His voice carried across the pizza shop. "Look who *jest* walked in!"

Pete and Penny ran out of the kitchen. The two men who had just come in were tall and thin.

"Hi, Rupert! Hi, Elliot!" Pete shouted. He gave them both high fives. Penny was right behind him.

"Hey, you two!" Elliot said.

"Whoa!" yelled Rupert, looking at his brother's hair. "Elliot, your hair!" Rupert pulled an envelope from his back pocket and swatted his brother's head with it.

"What was that for?" Elliot complained. He grabbed the envelope.

"Your hair was on fire," Rupert explained. "I had to put it out."

"Rupert, my hair is *always* fiery red," Elliot said as he patted down his crazy hair.

"Glad I don't have that problem," replied Rupert. He happily skimmed his hand over his shiny, bald head.

Pete and Penny laughed. So did their parents. Rupert and Elliot owned Redville's toy store, Jest Joking. They were always clowning around. Pete and Penny thought they were great. The brothers even hung out with them sometimes when Mr. and Mrs. Pizzarelli had errands to run. The Jests were silly, but they could be serious when they had to be.

"How'd the second day of the toy fair go?" Penny asked

as she led the brothers to their favorite booth.

"Great! This year's fair is the best yet," Rupert answered. "And check out our snazzy outfits!"

"Those vests with question marks on them are really cool," said Penny, pulling out her notepad. Pete stifled a laugh.

"Now, would you like your usual?" asked Penny.

The brothers nodded. Elliot always ordered a slice with sausage and green olives. Rupert liked pepperoni and black olives on his.

"Got it! They'll be up soon." Penny headed to the kitchen.

Just then, Pete noticed that a man wearing a cowboy hat had stepped into the pizza parlor. He was tall with dark hair and a bushy mustache. He took a seat in the booth right next to the Jests. Pete went over to take his order.

"Welcome to Pizzarelli's! What can I get for you?" asked Pete.

"I'd like a mushroom and pineapple slice and a large glass of milk," the stranger told him. Pete tried not to wrinkle his nose as he wrote down the man's weird order.

When he walked past the Jests' booth, Pete noticed them opening an envelope.

"Gosh, Rupert, you really crumpled that envelope when you swatted Elliot!" remarked Pete. "I hope it wasn't important."

"We're actually not sure what's inside," Elliot told him. "Someone stuck it under our door. It was there when we opened the shop this morning. We don't even know who it's from." Inside the envelope was a sheet of paper.

Pete sat down to peer at the paper with them. "It's a maze!" He could see the jumble of lines and the spot marked Start. He squinted to get a better look. The drawings were tiny. "Can I help you solve it?" Pete asked with excitement.

"Absolutely! You're way better at puzzles than we are!" Rupert handed a pencil to Pete. Elliot slid the maze over to him.

"Did I hear someone say *puzzles*?" asked Penny. She was holding their slices of pizza. She slid into the booth and nudged Pete so she could see, too. They worked on the maze while Rupert and Elliot dug into their slices.

Solve the maze.

(Answer, page 62.)

"There!" Pete traced the route through the maze. "It leads here," he said, pointing.

The Jest brothers studied the image. "That fountain's at the Topsy-Turvy Toys factory in Garden City," Rupert said. "See how it looks like it's upside down? Get it? It's topsy-turvy!"

"You're right," his brother agreed. "Hey, maybe this maze has to do with the big contest!"

Pete and Penny leaned forward. "A contest?"

"Yes, the Turn the Tables Contest!" the Jest brothers said at once.

"Each year, there's a contest at the fair," Rupert explained. "It's a chance for toy store *owners* to become toy *makers*. On the first day, owners drop off designs for a new toy at the contest booth. The owner of Topsy-Turvy Toys chooses the best design. If you win, you get a lot of money and your design becomes a *real* toy!"

"Wow!" Penny said. "You could be on to something! This maze does lead to that toy factory."

"Maybe," answered Elliot. "But it's too late to follow the maze tonight. We'll go tomorrow."

"There's Benny," Rupert said, pointing to a

man sitting in a nearby booth. Benny Grande owned Benny's Beans, Redville's coffee shop. "Let's ask him to watch the store for us."

"Good idea," Elliot agreed.

Pete and Penny walked over to Benny's booth with Rupert and Elliot. Benny's face lit up when he saw the Jests.

"Hi, guys! Isn't this pizza the best?" he asked, patting his round belly.

"It sure is! We were wondering, though, could you please watch the store for us tomorrow morning?" Rupert asked. "We have an errand to run, but should be back by lunchtime."

"Sure," Benny answered. "I'll just let my staff know where to find me."

"Here's a little something to show our thanks! Don't spend it all at Pizzarelli's!" said Elliot. He handed over a pink, million-dollar bill.

Benny laughed and pocketed the play money. Then he went back to eating his pizza.

The brothers looked at each other. Then Rupert said to Pete and Penny, "Could you two come with us tomorrow? There might be more puzzles to solve."

"That sounds great!" Penny said with a grin. "We'll check with our parents."

"I've never been to a toy factory!" Pete added.

"A toy factory, eh?" Mr. Pizzarelli walked over to the booth.

Rupert and Elliot explained about the maze. "We need their help," Elliot finished.

"Please, Dad," Pete said. "Can we?"

"All right," Mr. Pizzarelli said. "I know the Jests will keep an eye on you." He smiled. "And with them, I'm sure it'll be an adventure."

"We'll meet you out front tomorrow morning," Elliot told them as he and Rupert walked to the door. "Around ten."

"Great!" Penny said.

"Hey, kid!" It was the man in the cowboy hat. "Where's my pizza?"

Oops! Pete realized he had forgotten to put in the man's order. He'd been busy with the maze. "Sorry, coming right up!" he answered.

Pete rushed to the kitchen. When he glanced back, the man was watching him. And he did *not* seem happy. Pete didn't like the way the man was looking at him—not one bit.

Chapter Three

Pete and Penny were standing outside Pizzarelli's at ten the next morning. The brothers walked up a few minutes later.

"Good morning! Ready for another puzzling day?" joked Rupert.

"We sure are," said Pete and Penny.

"Where on earth did you find those ties?" Penny asked. "I love that they're covered in gumdrops!"

"We can't reveal our sources!" replied Elliot. Rupert nodded in agreement.

The four of them walked past Benny's Beans on the way to the parking lot.

"Hey, watch it!" a man snapped as he hurried out of the coffee shop. He'd almost run into Penny.

"You should really watch where *you're* going," Penny replied. "*You're* the one carrying a hot drink." The man stopped and glared at her. He was tall. His brown hair was cut short and was flat on top. He opened his mouth to say something, but—

"Hello, Mr. Buzz," Rupert said, quickly sticking out his hand.

Mr. Buzz shook Rupert's hand. *Bzzzt!* Rupert had a buzzer hidden in his palm. The Jests laughed—that is, until they noticed that coffee had spilled all over Mr. Buzz's suit jacket! Pete and Penny were wide-eyed.

"Look what you've done!" Mr. Buzz shouted. He dabbed at his suit jacket with a napkin. "Instead of playing pranks on me, you should be at the toy fair. You might learn a thing or two!" Then he walked away.

"He's not very friendly," Pete muttered.

"No, and he can't take a joke," Rupert agreed. "I mean, I'm sorry about his jacket. But, come on, buzzing Mr. *Buzz*—that's pretty funny!"

"How do you know that guy?" Penny asked, scrunching up her nose.

"He owns Groovy Games over in Bellville," said Elliot. "It's actually a really good toy store. It has a bigger selection of board games than Jest Joking."

The four of them got into the Jests' car. As they headed to Garden City, Pete asked, "So when were you last at the Topsy-Turvy Toys factory?"

"We were actually only there once—when we'd first opened our store," Rupert replied. Elliot was driving. "Ms. Zippy likes to give her new clients a factory tour so they can see where the toys are made."

"Ms. Zippy?" Penny asked. "That's a zippity-do-da name!"

"Well, she's a zippity-do-da lady who sure knows toys," Elliot agreed. "She owns Topsy-Turvy Toys. She's the person who chooses the winner of the Turn the Tables Contest each year."

"Do you buy all your toys from Topsy-Turvy Toys?" asked Pete.

"Almost," Rupert answered. "They make the best toys."

"If we win the contest this year, then *we'll* make the best toys," his brother pointed out.

Penny scratched her head. "Do you two enter the contest every year?"

"Yes," Elliot said. "And every year we get . . . The Letter."

"The rejection letter," Rupert explained. "If you enter the contest, you have to pick up a letter at the contest booth on the third night of the fair. You either get a rejection letter or a letter saying you've won."

"The third night . . . that's tonight!" Pete exclaimed.

"And when do they announce the winner to *everyone*?" Penny asked.

Rupert grinned. "Tomorrow, on the last day of the fair. There's a press conference where they reveal the winning toy. Then the winner signs a giant toy contract with a special feather pen. The time and location of the event are top secret, though. The winner and the press are the only people who know where and when it is. They receive special invitations."

Elliot snorted. "Mr. Buzz'll probably win again this year."

"Mr. Buzz *makes* toys, too?" Pete asked. "I mean, I know he runs a toy store, but how does a guy like that come up with fun ideas?"

"I don't know, but he *is* creative. He's won the Turn the Tables Contest the last three years in a row!" Rupert told them. He shook his head. "He's come up with very clever toy designs."

"So have we," Elliot insisted. "And this year's design is our best yet!"

"Well, this maze pointed us to the Topsy-Turvy Toys factory. And Topsy-Turvy Toys runs the toy contest," Pete said. "Maybe you really did win!"

Elliot tooted the car horn. "Yes, this could be our year!"

Pete asked Rupert if he could see the maze. *Maybe there's something on here about the contest,* he thought. Rupert passed it to him and Pete began looking for hidden clues.

Then he noticed something. He pulled out his magnifying glass and looked again. "Hey!" He nudged Penny. "Check this out!"

Penny followed his finger. "Yeah, so? We know that's the fountain."

"Look closer," Pete said. He patiently handed her the magnifying glass.

Penny squinted at the paper. She gasped. "There are markings in there!"

Rupert peered over his seat. "In where?"

"Inside the drawing of the fountain," Pete answered. "They could be letters."

Pete pulled out his notebook. He traced the tiny markings onto a blank page. Then he wrote them the same way, but larger, on a new page. That way, everyone could see them.

Rupert frowned. "S-e-l-a-c-s and r-e-d-n-u. Those letters look funny."

"Funny how?" Elliot asked. He was keeping his eyes on the road.

"Each letter looks backward," Pete said. He tore out the page and held it up for Rupert and Elliot to see. "See? It's hard to read."

Penny looked at the page and laughed. "You can't read that?"

Pete frowned. "No," he admitted. "Why? Can you?"

Hold this page up to a mirror to read the message.

(Answer, page 62.)

"Easy-peasy!" she bragged. She took the page from him. She turned it around and held it up for him to see.

Pete looked. Then he gasped. He could read the letters clearly from the flip side of the paper. The entire message had been written backward!

"Under scales," he read out loud. "Good work, Penny!" He laughed.

"Thanks! But what does that mean?" she asked.

"I don't have any idea," replied Rupert.

"I don't know, either," Pete said. "But I bet we'll find out at the fountain!"

"Are we almost to the factory?" asked Penny.

"We'll be there soon enough," answered Elliot. He pointed up ahead on the highway.

Pete looked out the car window. There was a sign for Garden City. *We must be getting close,* he thought. *I can't wait to see what we find next!*

Chapter Four

Whirr-toot!

"What was that?" Pete asked.

"That was the factory whistle," Rupert said. "We're almost there."

They turned a corner. The Topsy-Turvy Toys factory stretched out before them. "Wow," Pete said. Penny's mouth was open.

The factory was huge! There were three small buildings and one big one. They were all painted bright colors. There were spinning tops and whirligigs on their roofs. Whistles and whirs and bumps and bangs filled the air. Workers hurried about carrying boxes, papers, and, of course, toys! It was a constant blur of motion.

"Which way's the fountain?" Penny asked as they got out of the car.

"I remember it being over this way." Elliot led them between buildings to a green lawn.

A large stone fountain sat in the center. It was made to look like it had been built upside down. Even the water seemed to run in the wrong direction! Pete and Penny turned their heads to look at it right side up.

"Now what?" asked Penny.

"Remember the hidden words—*under scales*," Pete reminded her. "Those words must be a clue." They looked in and around the fountain.

"Here!" Penny called out. She had found carvings of animals all along the fountain's edges. She was pointing to one that looked like a fish. "Scales! Get it? Like the skin of a fish!"

"Of course!" They all hurried to that spot. Pete looked beneath where the fish's tail hung over the side of the fountain. Something glittered in the water.

"I see something!" He reached in and pulled out a small object in a plastic bag.

"It's a tiny key!" said Penny. Pete handed the key to Rupert.

"What's this other thing?" Rupert asked. A small disk was tied to the key.

"That's a cipher disk!" Pete said. "It's used to

crack coded messages." He pointed to it. "See, it has two sets of letters. You swap each letter for the one lined up next to it. That gives you the answer. Usually you can spin the disk to change the code, but this one is lined up for us."

"And ours has a coded message on it!" Penny added. She pointed to the back of the disk.

"Can you two solve it?" Elliot asked. Pete and Penny put their heads together to figure it out.

Decode the message. (Use the secret code in the front of this book!)

(Answer, page 62.)

ITVY YIF
_ _ _ _   _ _ _
IFBSA MFZYVRZ
_ _ _ _ _   _ _ _ _ _ _ _
YTL NFAY
_ _ _   _ _ _ _
OLYYLBA?
_ _ _ _ _ _ _?

Pete copied the letters into his notebook. He and Penny used the disk to translate the message. "Hmm," Pete said after reading the riddle out loud.

"We'll never figure that out!" Penny said.

Rupert was holding the key. "I wonder what this opens . . . If we can find the right keyhole, maybe we won't need to solve the riddle."

"Good thinking!" said Pete. "Can I have a look?" Pete studied the key. "There's a number on it: three hundred fourteen. So there must be a door somewhere with that number on it. Maybe it opens a door right here at the factory. Let's look around!"

Elliot glanced at his watch. "But we promised Benny we'd be back by lunchtime."

"And I'm starving!" Rupert clutched his stomach. He grabbed the end of Elliot's tie and chewed on it.

"Hey, eat your own gumdrops!" Elliot told him. He yanked his tie back. Then he took a small nibble of it himself. "Hmm. Not bad."

"We should at least look for the keyhole while we're here. It should be easy to recognize since it will be so tiny," Pete remarked. "We can head back to Redville after that."

They all started searching.

Penny headed toward the biggest building. "I bet it's inside this one," she said. She pulled the door open. "Come on!"

Pete sighed and followed her. He tended to get a bad feeling whenever Penny jumped into something. Rupert and Elliot came along.

Inside were two hallways with shiny, wooden floors and wacky pictures on the walls. There were doorways that led to fancy offices. "There are people working in here," Pete whispered. "We need to be super quiet." Pete and Penny started tiptoeing down one long hallway. Elliot and Rupert headed down the other.

Pete and Penny heard whispered voices. They were coming from an open office doorway. The nameplate on the door said Ms. ZIPPY. Penny couldn't help looking in . . .

A tall woman with short, curly hair stood in front of a huge, wooden desk. She was talking quietly to a man in coveralls smudged with ink. She kept glancing around as she spoke, as though she were telling a secret. "So we just need to—," she said. Then she spotted Penny peering in the doorway!

"Can I help you?" the woman asked. Her eyebrows were raised. *This has to be Ms. Zippy*, thought Penny.

The man started toward Penny. "Well, answer her," he demanded.

"I was just, uh, looking for the bathroom!" Penny blurted out. It was the first thing she could think of.

Ms. Zippy frowned and glanced past Penny to Pete. "Who are you? Where are your parents?"

"I really have to find the bathroom. It's an emergency!" Penny said, bouncing up and down. Then she yanked the door shut. "Run!" she mouthed to Pete. They raced down the hall and waved at the Jests to follow them. There was a big door ahead of them and Penny pulled it open. They all dashed through and slammed it shut behind them. The sun was shining.

"Phew!" Pete said. He was breathing hard.

"Why are we running?" asked Rupert.

"We saw Ms. Zippy, and let's just say she was

not happy when she saw us!" said Pete.

"Yeah, she was whispering about something just before she spotted us," Penny added. "It all seemed awfully suspicious!"

"Hurry! We should leave before Ms. Zippy comes after us!" said Pete.

They walked away from the door and almost ran into a woman who was rushing past them. She was holding lots of papers.

"Oh!" The woman saw the four of them and stumbled. Her papers went flying. "I'm sorry!" She was slim with blond hair that flipped up at the ends. She had a big, lavender flower tucked behind her left ear. The woman scurried to pick up the papers as the wind whirled them around. Pete, Penny, and the Jests helped her.

"No problem," Pete said. "Here you go." He handed the woman some crinkled papers.

"Here's another," Penny told her. "By the way—cool dress." It was bright purple with small pink tulips all over it.

"Oh, thanks. I felt very purple today. Don't you ever feel like a particular color? I know I do. Today was definitely a purple day." The woman clutched her papers and hurried away.

"She seemed nervous," Elliot said.

Penny saw a paper caught behind a bush. She picked it up. It was a note, but she didn't have time to read it. Penny quickly folded the paper and stuck it in her pocket. *That woman was jittery,* she thought. *I wonder why . . . Could this note be a clue?*

Pete saw what Penny had done. He shook his head. "Can we just get out of here?" he urged.

"None of us found any tiny keyholes," Penny replied. "But—" She heard a door opening. Ms. Zippy was rushing toward them.

"Run!" yelled Pete.

Rupert and Elliot raced to the parking lot. Pete and Penny ran as fast as they could to keep up. They all piled into the car.

As they drove away, Penny glanced back. Ms. Zippy was standing there, hands on her hips. She didn't look happy. Penny couldn't help thinking, *We made it out just in time!*

Chapter Five

Penny was tearing her napkin up into tiny pieces. "I don't get this riddle," she said. *"What two words contain the most letters?"*

They were all eating lunch together at Jest Joking. Benny was there, too. He had gone to check on his shop and brought back sandwiches for everyone.

Pete shrugged. "Together, I'm sure we can think up lots of long words," he answered. "Let's start making a list." Pete took out a pencil and his notebook. Everyone made suggestions.

"*Adventurous* and *hippopotamus* are long words," suggested Penny.

"How about *fantastical imagination*," Benny said.

"Or *scrumptious confectionary*?" Rupert offered.

"I know! I know!" said Elliot. "It's got to be *superduperdiddleyumpty tudiniferous!*"

Pete laughed. "Those aren't real words!"

"The riddle did not say 'what two *real* words,'" replied Elliot.

"We need a dictionary," Penny muttered.

Just then, the door chime rang. "Hello, Jests!" a voice called out. A man stepped inside. He wore a blue jacket and a blue cap. He carried a large canvas bag filled with mail.

"Mr. Parcel!" Pete and Penny called out.

"Well, hello, young Pizzarellis!" Mr. Parcel replied. He placed mail on the counter. "I didn't expect to see *you* here." When Mr. Parcel delivered mail to the pizza parlor, he often brought a riddle for Pete and Penny to solve.

Penny snapped her fingers. *Mr. Parcel was great at giving riddles,* she thought. *Maybe he can solve them, too!* "We actually have a riddle for *you* today!" She glanced at Rupert and Elliot. They both nodded.

"Really?" Mr. Parcel rubbed his hands together. "Let's hear it!"

"What two words contain the most letters?" Penny recited the riddle from the fountain.

Mr. Parcel thought for a minute. Then, to everyone's surprise, he laughed. "Oh, that's easy! *Post* and *office*—the post office!"

"You're a genius!" Rupert said. He pulled the tiny key out of his pocket. He handed it to the mailman. "Then this key must open a post-office box!"

Mr. Parcel studied the tiny key. "Yep, it's for one of our boxes," he replied. "Box three hundred fourteen." He pointed to the number on the key.

"Let's go!" Elliot shouted. "Uh, Benny?"

"Don't worry about it," Benny answered. "I'll watch the shop until you get back."

"Thanks!" Elliot ran outside. The others followed him.

"Good luck!" Mr. Parcel called after them as they raced down the street. Fortunately the post office was only a few blocks away.

Penny reached the post office first. She went to open the door and was almost knocked over by a woman who was rushing out. "Pardon me," the woman said. She was wearing a big hat decorated with yellow flowers along the brim. Penny couldn't see the woman's face under the big, floppy hat, but something about her seemed familiar. The woman hurried off.

Pete and the Jests caught up to Penny. "Let's find that box!" Elliot said. He led the way into the post office.

The post-office boxes took up one wall. Pete scanned the numbers. *It's got to be here somewhere,* thought Pete. "Here it is!" he called out. He pointed to the right box.

Rupert inserted the key and turned it. The little door opened. Inside was a piece of paper.

"Look!" Rupert unfolded it. Elliot, Pete, and Penny all peered over his shoulder.

"It looks like we'll need the cipher disk again," Pete said. Rupert handed it to him. Pete took out his notebook and pencil. "Let's see if we can puzzle it out."

He wrote down the jumbled letters and read them out to Penny. Penny read the corresponding letters back to him from on the cipher disk.

Decode the message. (Use the secret code in the front of this book!)

(Answer, page 62.)

ZFFZ   BMM   RZHF

____   ___   ____

SLAP   AKZSVX

____   _____

Then Pete wrote the correct letter below each coded letter in the message.

"Noon RCC info desk Sunday," he read out.

"Huh?" asked Penny.

"I've got it!" shouted Elliot. "RCC is the Redville Convention Center! We must need to be at the information desk there at noon on Sunday—that's tomorrow!"

His brother pinched him on the arm. "This

could be about the Turn the Tables Contest!"

"You could be right," Elliot said. He rubbed his arm. "The toy fair is at the RCC. Pete, Penny, make sure your parents are okay with you coming along again. We still need your help!"

"Of course!" Penny said. "We should hurry home, though. Mom and Dad will want to hear what we've been up to all day."

"And *we* should make our way to the RCC now to pick up our letter from the contest booth," said Elliot. "Keep your fingers crossed that the letter says we've won!"

"Okay, good luck! See you at twelve o'clock tomorrow," Pete told the Jests.

"I wonder what these puzzles are all about," Mr. Pizzarelli said as he looked over the maze and cipher-disk messages.

"It's good of you to help Rupert and Elliot. I just hope this doesn't lead to any sort of trouble," said Mrs. Pizzarelli.

"We know you'll be safe with the Jests," Mr. Pizzarelli added. "So you kids can go tomorrow, too. Just be careful."

That night, when Penny sat down on her bed to take off her sneakers, she felt something in her back pocket. It was the paper the nervous woman had dropped at the factory. Penny had totally forgotten about it! She unfolded the paper and read it.

Memo

Flora,
    Have my suit
    cleaned by 11:00am

Mr. Buzz

She folded the paper up again. Then she slid it into the jeans she'd set out for the next day. *Maybe the nervous woman from the factory was the "Flora" in this note? But why was she at the factory? Could this note possibly be a clue?* thought Penny. She wasn't sure. But she knew she didn't trust anyone connected with Mr. Buzz!

Chapter Six

"Have fun!" said Mrs. Pizzarelli as she dropped Pete and Penny off at the convention center the next day. The Jests waved to Pete and Penny. But they weren't smiling.

"Oh no! Did you get The Letter?" Pete asked, running to them.

Elliot's shoulders sagged. He tugged on his striped bow tie. "Yes. We got a *rejection* letter last night," he explained. "Our design didn't win."

"Oh. I'm sorry." Penny patted Rupert's back.

"I bet Mr. Buzz won—again." Rupert sighed. "One thing is weird, though. Ms. Zippy didn't give back our toy design. In the past, she's always returned it with The Letter."

"Well, try not to think about that right now," Pete urged. "There's still a mystery to solve! We have to keep following the clues."

"Pete's right," agreed Penny. "We may not

know where these clues are taking us, but they could lead to something great. Right?"

The brothers nodded. The group headed inside.

Pete and Penny had never been inside the convention center before. There were people everywhere. And toys! The lobby had maps of booth locations posted everywhere. A big, round desk stood in the center. The sign above the desk read INFORMATION.

"Hello, I'm Elliot Jest," Elliot told the girl sitting there. "Do you have a message for me?"

She looked through a stack of envelopes and smiled. "Yes, here it is." She handed him an envelope. It had *Jest* written on it.

Elliot opened the envelope. It held a single piece of paper. There were four rows of pictures on it. Elliot shrugged. He gave Penny the paper.

"It's a rebus!" Pete shouted as he crowded beside her.

Elliot frowned. "What's that?"

"It's a puzzle made of pictograms—when you use pictures to form words," explained Pete. He and Penny started studying the rebus.

39

"There's a knee in the first row," Penny said. "And *knee* minus *kn* leaves *ee*. So *m* plus *ee* would sound like *me*."

"Great! And the second row shows what looks like a person blowing out air," Pete replied. "And that's a bee. So *blow* minus *b* leaves *low*."

"And the letter *d* is what's missing from the third row!" exclaimed Penny.

"*Me, low, d,*" Pete said. "*Melody?*"

"Melody!" Elliot and Rupert smiled. "That's the name of one of the meeting rooms here," Rupert explained to Pete and Penny. Then he looked at the note again. "And that clock drawing shows twelve fifteen. It's almost that time now! Let's go!"

They raced up a big staircase. Each of the doors along the back hall was marked with a plaque. The fourth door's plaque said MELODY.

"Here we are!" Elliot rubbed his hands together. He pulled the door open. "It sure is crowded!" They all looked inside.

The Melody Room was fancy. There were heavy curtains along the walls. The floor had thick, orange carpeting. Cushy chairs were lined up facing a long, polished wooden table at the front. Lots of big cameras were up front, too.

"What are all these people doing here?" Pete asked as they stepped inside. "Do you think they all found puzzles, too?"

"Maybe," Rupert replied.

Penny nudged Pete. "Look!" She pointed. "It's the guy in the cowboy hat who we saw at the pizza parlor!" Sure enough, the man was there. He was scribbling something in a small notebook.

"And there's Ms. Scoop!" Pete gestured toward the reporter from the *Redville Gazette*. She was sitting in the back row.

"Ms. Scoop wrote that story about us when we solved the Case of the Secret Sauce," Penny reminded the Jests. They nodded.

"I see Mr. Buzz." Rupert gestured toward the table at the front. Mr. Buzz was looking around the room. When he saw Rupert pointing at him, he turned pale. Then he turned bright red and balled his hands into fists by his sides.

"It looks like he's still upset about the buzzer," Elliot said. "And it's crowded so we'll have to stand in the back."

Ms. Scoop turned and smiled at the kids.
"What are you two doing here?" she asked.

"We're not exactly sure. What's all this for?"
Penny asked.

"Ms. Zippy is about to announce the Turn
the Tables Contest winner," Ms. Scoop told her.
"But you really shouldn't be here without an
official top secret invitation."

"We were sort of invited," Pete replied.
Ms. Scoop was interested in hearing more, but
everyone suddenly got very quiet. A tall woman
had stepped up to the table. It was Ms. Zippy.

"Thank you all for coming," Ms. Zippy said
as she looked around the room. Pete noticed
Ms. Zippy's eyes widen as soon as she saw him
and his sister. "As you know, today we will
announce the winner of this year's Turn the
Tables Contest. And, as always, we want *the press*
to hear it first."

"If the Jests didn't win the contest and these
people are all reporters," Pete whispered to
Penny, "then what are *we* doing here?"

Penny shushed him.

"The wait is over," Ms. Zippy continued. "This year's Turn the Tables Contest winner is . . . Mr. Bill Buzz!"

Mr. Buzz stepped onstage. He was wearing a brightly colored necktie. "Thank you, this is a true honor. But I think I spilled something on my tie! Have a look, would you?" he asked.

Ms. Zippy tugged at his tie for a closer look—and it suddenly lit up! Music played as the tie curled up and around into a ball.

"Ladies and gentlemen," Ms. Zippy announced, smiling, "I give you the newest Topsy-Turvy toy—the BuzzBall!"

Everyone *ooh*ed and *aah*ed. But Pete heard Rupert and Elliot gasp beside him.

"That's *our* toy!" Rupert said softly.

"What do you mean?" Penny asked.

"That's our toy design!" Elliot agreed. "The one we submitted to the contest!"

Ms. Zippy continued, "As you can see, this is an ordinary necktie until you pull on it. Then it rolls up. You unhook the loop from your neck and slide it over the ball like a sleeve. And— ta-da!—you have the BuzzBall! It lights up and plays music, too."

"School picture day will never be the same again!" Mr. Buzz pointed out, laughing.

Then he and Ms. Zippy tossed the BuzzBall back and forth. Everyone clapped.

"He stole our design!" Elliot insisted to Pete.

"He must've somehow taken it from the Turn the Tables Contest booth," Rupert guessed.

"Yes. He must have swiped our design and put his name on it!" agreed Elliot.

"Can you prove it?" Pete asked.

"Yes—no." Elliot groaned. "Ms. Zippy didn't return our original design drawing, remember? All we got was The Letter." He shoved the rejection letter at Penny.

"But we have a photocopy of the design. It's back at our shop," Rupert reminded him.

"That's right! We'll have to go get it—and fast! We need to be back here before Mr. Buzz signs *our* toy contract!" Elliot said. He and Rupert glanced at Pete and Penny.

Ms. Scoop must have been listening because she turned toward them all and said, "Another mystery? I might have known!" She smiled at Pete and Penny. "You two can stay with me until Rupert and Elliot get back."

"Great!" the Jests said. "We won't be long." They glared at Mr. Buzz and then rushed out.

Chapter Seven

Dear Rupert and Elliot Jest,

Thank you for submitting your design to the Turn the Tables Contest.

Unfortunately, it was not selected as this year's winner. Better luck next year!

Sincerely,

Ms. Zippy

Penny unfolded the rejection letter Elliot had handed her and read it. Something about it was bugging her. But what?

"All the clues led us here so that the Jests would find out that Mr. Buzz stole their toy design . . . ," said Pete.

"It sure looks that way," his sister agreed.

"But if someone wanted the Jests to know about the theft, why not just tell them? Who would've sent these clues?"

Pete and Penny studied the crowd.

"Maybe *he* sent the clues," Pete suggested.

Look carefully. Who's been sending the clues?

(Answer, page 62.)

He pointed to the man in the cowboy hat. "He was in the booth beside us when the Jests first showed us the maze. And now he's here."

Penny shook her head. "But we really don't know anything about that guy. Hey, do you have the maze?"

"Yep." Pete pulled it out of his pocket. "I've even got this." He held up the cipher disk.

Penny looked at the disk. "It's strange that this cipher disk is not a perfect circle. Most are," she noticed. "See how this one dips in at the edges? Almost like a flower—"

Pete's eyes got wide. "That's it!" He took the maze from Penny. "The maze has a flower on it, too! See the doodle up in the corner?"

Penny looked at the info desk note. "And look! There are flowers on this paper, too!"

She and Pete looked at each other. "Whoever sent these clues must have a thing for flowers," Penny said. "That means—"

"The nervous woman!" Pete said.

"That's exactly who I thought of!" Penny exclaimed. "At the factory, she was wearing a dress with tulips all over it!"

"And a flower in her hair!" added Pete.

They looked around the room. *She must be here somewhere*, they thought. *There!* The nervous woman was sitting up front. She was wearing a daisy-print sundress and a daisy-shaped hairpin. When she saw Pete and Penny looking at her, she gasped. She jumped to her feet and headed toward the exit.

"She's running to the door! It must be her!" Pete whispered to his sister.

"We can't let her get away!" Penny replied. They rushed toward the woman. Penny blocked her path before she could reach the door.

"You sent those clues!" Penny accused. She remembered the note. "Are you *Flora*?"

"Yes, that's me. I'm Flora, Flora Faint," the woman admitted.

Pete looked at Penny. "How did you know her name?" he asked.

"Remember the note I found at the factory? The one I kept . . . ," Penny said sheepishly.

"Yes," said Pete.

"Well, it was a note to someone named Flora—from Mr. Buzz!" explained Penny.

"I am Mr. Buzz's assistant," said Flora.

"His assistant?" Pete glared at her. "Did you help steal the Jests' toy design?"

"No!" Flora said. "I saw Mr. Buzz take the design from the booth. I had to tell the Jests what had happened. But if Mr. Buzz got away with it, and found out I said something, he would fire me. And he'd make it so other toy stores wouldn't hire me, either." She glanced around. "I read the *Redville Gazette* article about the 'Case of the Secret Sauce.' I hoped that if I left puzzles you'd help the Jests decipher them. That way I could tell the truth without having to say anything directly."

"That's why you were at the factory—you were leaving the cipher disk and key," Pete guessed.

"And that was you at the post office, too? In the flowery hat?" added Penny.

"Yes." Flora nodded. "I had to change the message at the post office. Originally I was only going to tell you Mr. Buzz had stolen the Jests' design. But when the design actually won, I had to find a way to tell you about this top secret event." She glanced quickly toward the front table. She started wringing her hands.

"Now you have to tell Ms. Zippy that Mr. Buzz is a thief," Penny begged.

Flora shook her head. "I can't! I'll lose my job! I'm so sorry!" She pushed past them and ran out the door.

"Now what?" Pete asked his sister.

Penny started to reply. Then she felt inside her pocket. The paper Flora had dropped at the factory! *Flora hadn't dropped it on purpose*, thought Penny. *But it might be just what they needed!*

Chapter Eight

Penny quickly pulled Flora's note from her pocket. She held it up beside the rejection letter. "That's it!" Penny whispered. "I knew something was weird about this rejection letter!"

Pete looked at Penny, eyebrows raised.

"The signatures!" Penny waved the note at him. "Look at the signatures!"

Pete studied them—and gasped. "Those z's look exactly the same!"

"Exactly!" Penny glanced around. "Where are the Jests?"

"Not back yet. And I don't think we can wait," Pete told her. He pointed. Ms. Zippy had just handed Mr. Buzz the giant toy contract and a fancy feather pen.

"Oh no! The contract!" Penny said. "If he signs that contract, everyone will believe it's his design! Come on!" She pushed through the crowd to the front of the room. Pete was right behind her. Ms. Scoop followed them.

Mr. Buzz set the contract on the table. He flipped to the last page, pen in hand.

"Stop!" Penny shouted as loud as she could. Everyone turned to stare at her. "This man is a thief!" She pointed at Mr. Buzz. "He did not design the BuzzBall!"

"That's ridiculous!" Mr. Buzz said. He crossed his arms.

"I'm sorry, children, but you're mistaken," Ms. Zippy argued. "Mr. Buzz designed the BuzzBall. I have his original design in my bag."

"The Jest brothers turned in that design," Pete said. "Mr. Buzz stole it from the contest booth. He somehow removed their names and put his own on it instead."

Ms. Zippy shook her head. "The Jests? They didn't even enter the contest this year."

Mr. Buzz laughed. "Kids and their stories!" He glared at Pete and Penny. Then he leaned down. He whispered into Pete's ear: "Just try to prove it." Pete stepped back.

Penny set the note and the letter on the

table—right on top of the contract. "This is the rejection letter the Jests picked up from the contest booth last night," she explained to the crowd. "And this is a note Mr. Buzz wrote to his assistant. Look at the handwriting!"

Ms. Zippy leaned over and examined the two papers. Her eyes widened. "This isn't my signature!" she exclaimed. "I didn't even send the Jests a letter. In fact, I was surprised they hadn't entered this year. They always have in the past. And that *is* the same writing! So if Mr. Buzz signed that note, then he also signed this rejection letter." Ms. Zippy held up the letter and glared at Mr. Buzz. He backed away.

Just then, Rupert and Elliot rushed into the room. Ms. Scoop turned to Penny. "I'll be right back," she said.

"Here's a photocopy of our original design," Rupert said. He handed it to Ms. Zippy.

She reviewed it. Then she pulled the design entry out from her bag. They were exactly the same. Only hers had Mr. Buzz's name on it.

"They *are* the same design," Ms. Zippy announced. "Mr. Buzz really did steal it!"

Dear Ra...... Elliot Jest,

Thank you for submitting
your design to the Turn the
Tables Contest.
Unfortunately, it was not
selected as this year's
winner. Better luck next
year!

Sincerely,

Ms. Zippy

Contract

Oohs filled the crowded room. Cameras flashed. Mr. Buzz glanced toward the exit. Suddenly, he darted for the door. But a large hand grabbed him by the collar!

"I'll take care of this! It's a good thing I was nearby," a strong voice said. Pete and Penny turned. It was Captain Bell, the chief of police. Ms. Scoop was right behind him. She must have gone to get him.

"You're under arrest," Captain Bell told Mr. Buzz.

"How could you steal the Jests' toy design, Mr. Buzz?" Ms. Zippy asked.

Mr. Buzz hung his head. "I needed money for my shop. And I couldn't think of a good toy design this year," he admitted. "When I saw the Jests drop off their toy design, I realized it was a winner. I just had to have it!"

"I'm very disappointed," Ms. Zippy stated. Captain Bell led Mr. Buzz away.

Then Ms. Zippy turned to Rupert and Elliot. "I'm sorry about all of this. I had no idea."

"Neither did we," Elliot replied. "Not until someone sent us cryptic clues."

"Clues? Is that why you were at the factory?" Ms. Zippy asked. "When these kids walked into my office, I was talking to my foreman about the BuzzBall's top secret prototype. I wanted to make sure you hadn't overheard anything—or swear you to secrecy if you had."

"We thought you were going to call the police on us!" Penny replied.

"Not at all," said Ms. Zippy, shaking her head. "Well, I still think the BuzzBall is great! Would you accept my apologies—and my congratulations on being the real contest winners?" she asked the Jests. Cameras flashed.

Rupert and Elliot grinned. "Absolutely!" they said together. "And just so you know, we named it the TieBall."

Pete and Penny were overjoyed that the mystery had been solved. "This calls for a party!"

Pete grinned. "Yeah, a *pizza* party!"

That night, Mr. and Mrs. Pizzarelli threw a party at Pizzarelli's. Everyone was there: the Jests, Ms. Zippy, Ms. Scoop, Captain Bell, Mr. Parcel, Benny, the man in the cowboy hat, and lots of reporters. Even Flora turned up! Captain Bell told her she wasn't in trouble. In fact, because of Mr. Buzz's ruined reputation, he'd have to sell Groovy Games. Flora had been saving up for her own toy shop. So now she could buy Groovy Games and run it herself!

"I can't believe Mr. Buzz thought he'd get away with this," Ms. Zippy said.

Captain Bell shook his head. "Well, he certainly hadn't counted on you two!" He looked at Pete and Penny.

"This mystery wouldn't have been solved without you!" the man in the cowboy hat added. He offered his hand. "Tim Columns. I'm a reporter for the *Bellville Ledger*."

"Bellville?" Rupert looked at the man. "That's where Mr. Buzz is from."

"Yes," Mr. Columns agreed. "I came to Redville to cover the toy fair—and to see if Mr. Buzz could win the Turn the Tables Contest four years in a row." He smiled. "Looks like the tables were turned on *him* this year!"

"This makes a great story," Ms. Scoop agreed. "I'm writing it up for the *Redville Gazette*. In fact, I've made the crossword right on my napkin!"

Use the clues to solve the puzzle.

(Answer, page 62.)

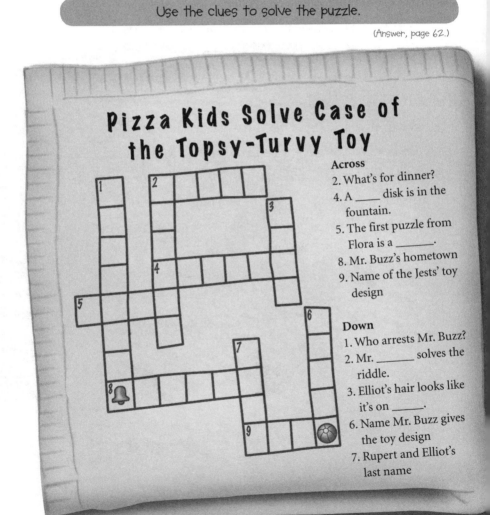

Pizza Kids Solve Case of the Topsy-Turvy Toy

Across

2. What's for dinner?
4. A _____ disk is in the fountain.
5. The first puzzle from Flora is a _____.
8. Mr. Buzz's hometown
9. Name of the Jests' toy design

Down

1. Who arrests Mr. Buzz?
2. Mr. _____ solves the riddle.
3. Elliot's hair looks like it's on _____.
6. Name Mr. Buzz gives the toy design
7. Rupert and Elliot's last name

"Good detective work, kids." Their dad gave them both a big hug. Their mom joined in.

Penny grinned. "What can I say? I guess we're Redville's official puzzle experts!"

"We *do* love puzzles," Pete agreed. "And I'm glad we could help the Jests."

Rupert handed Pete the TieBall prototype. "Here's something to show you our thanks for catching the toy thief!" he said.

Elliot stepped forward to shake Penny's hand. He added, "Yeah, you really nabbed Mr.—" *Bzzzt!*

Penny's hand tingled from the buzzer. She smiled and shook her head. Everyone laughed.

Pete grinned. "Know what I love just as much as puzzles—and the Jests' pranks?" he asked.

"What?" replied Mrs. Pizzarelli.

Pete grabbed a slice of pepperoni pizza.

"This!" he said. Then he opened his mouth and took a great big, cheesy bite.

Answer Page

Page 5

= 11

= 20

Page 10

Page 20

under scales

Page 24

ITVY YIF
WHAT TWO
IFBSA MFZYVRZ
WORDS CONTAIN
YTL NFAY
THE MOST
OLYYLBA?
LETTERS?

Page 34

ZFFZ   BMM   RZHF
NOON   RCC   INFO

SLAP   AKZSVX
DESK   SUNDAY

Page 39

M+(🐝-kn)

🐝 - 🐝

ABC_E

🕐

Melody 12:15

Page 47

Page 60

CAPTAIN
PIZZA
PARCEL
FIRE
CIPHER
MAZE
JESTIE
VILLE
BUZZ